Bunbun
at Bedtime

Sharon Pierce McCullough

Barefoot Books
better books for children

It's time
for
Bunbun
to go
to bed.

His big brother Benny puts away the toys.

His little sister Bibi makes a snack.

Bunbun
and
Paco
are
hiding.

Bunbun doesn't want to go to bed.

Benny and Bibi brush their teeth.

Bunbun is playing.

Benny and Bibi
put their clothes
in the hamper.

Bunbun is
still playing.

Splish!

Benny and Bibi

Splash!

take a bath.

Bunbun still doesn't want to go to bed.

Creak!

Suddenly, Bunbun hears a strange noise.

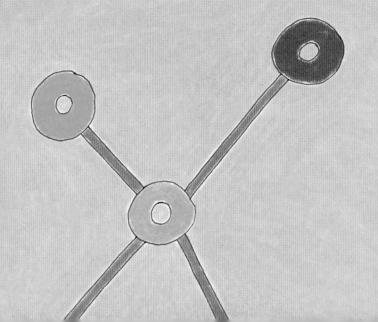

Bunbun is scared.

He runs
upstairs.

He
brushes
his
teeth.

He jumps
in the
bath.

He puts
on his
pajamas.

He
leaps
into
bed.

Goodnight, Bunbun!

For Ryan, my "night owl"

Barefoot Books
37 West 17th Street
4th Floor East
New York, NY 10011

Text and illustrations copyright © 2001 by Sharon Pierce McCullough
The moral right of Sharon Pierce McCullough to be identified as the
author and the illustrator of this work has been asserted

This book is printed on 100% acid-free paper
The illustrations were prepared in
Prisma color pencils on Bristol Board
Graphic design by Jennie Hoare, England
Typeset in 58pt Providence-Sans Bold
Color separation by Bright Arts, Singapore
Printed and bound in Hong Kong by
South China Printing Co. (1988) Ltd.

U.S. Cataloging-in-Publication Data
(Library of Congress Standards)

McCullough, Sharon Pierce.
Bunbun at bedtime / Sharon Pierce McCullough. — 1st. ed.
[32] p. : col. ill. ; 17 cm.
Summary: It is time for bed, but Bunbun is not tired. While his
brother and his sister go through their nightly bedtime rituals,
Bunbun stays downstairs to have a little nighttime fun of his own.
1. Rabbits — Fiction. 1. Title.
 [E] 21 2001 AC   CIP

1-84148-438-5

1 3 5 7 9 8 6 4 2

Barefoot Books
better books for children